ZZZZZZZZz

The Lion and the Mice

by **Rebecca Emberley**
and **Ed Emberley**

Holiday House / New York

Printed and Bound in April 2011 at Tien Wah Press, Johor Bahru, Johor, Malaysia.
The text typeface is Shannon Book.
The artwork was created digitally and with cut paper.
www.holidayhouse.com
First Edition
1 3 5 7 9 10 8 6 4 2

Library of Congress Cataloging-in-Publication Data
Emberley, Rebecca.
The lion and the mice / by Rebecca Emberley
and Ed Emberley. — 1st ed.
p. cm. — (I like to read)
Summary: A proud lion learns that
little mice can be his friends.
ISBN 978-0-8234-2357-6 (hardcover)
[1. Lion—Fiction. 2. Mice—Fiction.
3. Size—Fiction.] I. Emberley, Ed. II. Title.
PZ7.E5665Li 2011
[E]—dc22
2010044205

The lion sleeps.

The mouse is stuck.
She is lost.

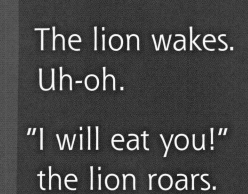

The lion wakes.
Uh-oh.

"I will eat you!"
the lion roars.

"No," the mouse begs.
"Do not eat me.
I am lost."

The lion lifts the mouse.
She sees her house.

"One day
I will help you,"
says the mouse.

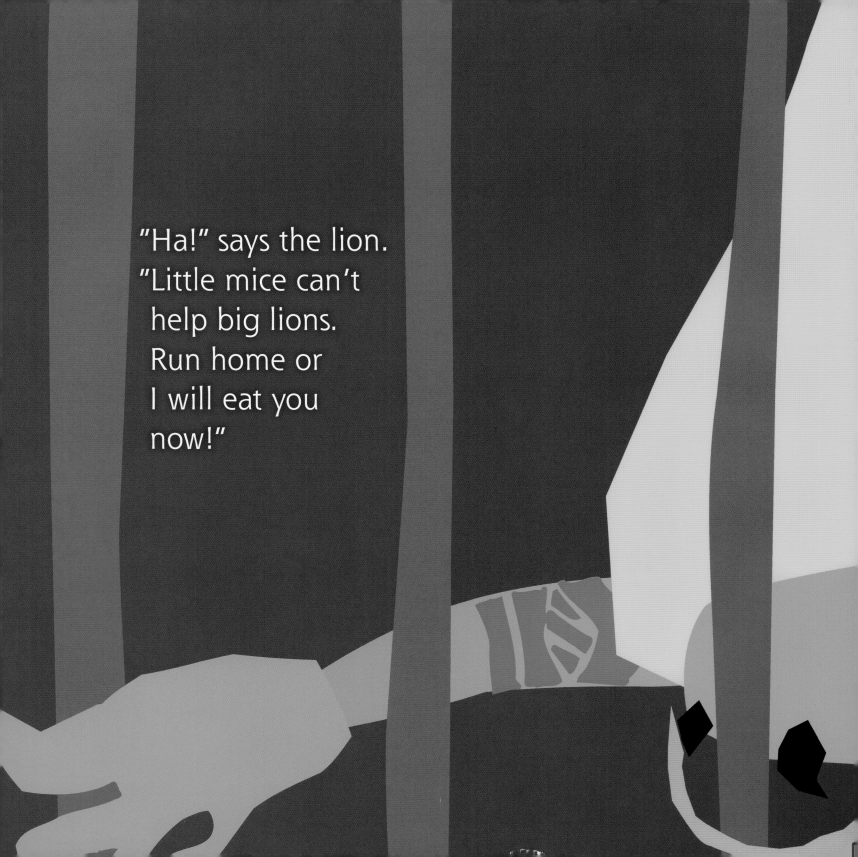

"Ha!" says the lion.
"Little mice can't
help big lions.
Run home or
I will eat you
now!"

The mouse runs home.

The lion sleeps.

The mouse
comes back.
More mice
come.
The lion roars.

"We will help you," say the mice.

They open the cage.

The lion is free.
The mice are
happy.

"See?" says the mouse.
"Little mice can be
big friends."